Rodgerhath and the Goldenaxe

Edward White

Cover Illustration by
Karen Luke

Chapter One

"One day," Stronghath the dwarf blacksmith exclaimed, "one day and you have broken it already."

"You should have made a better axe," Rodgerhath taunted in response.

"There was nothing wrong with that axe," Stronghath replied. "But I saw your sloppy swings on those logs and I might remind you that a war axe is not meant for splitting wood."

"I had no choice."

"Oh, how come?" Stronghath asked, an eyebrow raised.

"... my woodcutting axe is also broken."

Stronghath both sighed and laughed with his face.

"I can fix your axes next week."

"Next week!" Rodgerhath said, unamused. "I need it tomorrow. Are the years finally catching with you?" He gibed playfully. Despite the age gap, Rodgerhath and Stronghath had been friends for years and such banter was their normal dialect.

Stronghath laughed aloud.

"The only thing that's catching up with me are the dozen orders I've accepted that need to be done by the week's end. Your axes will have to wait."

Rodgerhath grumbled and cursed internally. There was nothing to be done, if his friend had work, he had work.

"I'm sure I'll manage until then. Farewell my friend."

The blacksmith bid him goodbye and Rodgerhath started the short stroll home. It was his custom – especially when he was in a bad mood – to stop at the brewery which

1

was owned by his father-in-law. He saw him outside the building holding a keg.

A promising sight for a beer lover such as himself. "Culbert!"

"Rodgerhath my dear son-in-law!" the brewer replied, scratching his greying beard. "How has life been treating you?"

"All is well but my axe is broken."

Culbert laughed.

"A completely normal day then! Well this should cheer you up," he said, scratching his big red nose, "I have finished another batch. I've imported new hops from Heresford and I've been using a dark-roasted barley for flavour. Take this keg and tell me what you think."

"With pleasure."

*

The beer was indeed a great pleasure. It tasted smoky because of the dark malt, but it had a certain levity as well because of the Heresford hops which Rodgerhath guessed had been applied liberally during the boil.

Whatever the case for the strange flavour, Rodgerhath enjoyed the strong brown ale immensely.

"Another triumph from your father!" Rodgerhath said, slamming his fist on the dining table, "although perhaps he should have left it to ferment longer to give the barley a chance to further darken the taste."

His wife, Flowergem, did not answer him. Rodgerhath did his best to ensure he only went on drinking sprees twice a week but he often broke this rule whenever he had a rough day or his father-in-law gave him ale to try.

Flowergem did not take kindly to Rodgerhath's indulgences and she had gone to bed, upon noting this was the fourth over-indulgence that week.

Rodgerhath didn't notice her absence such was his focus on the ale.

"Ah," he sighed, scratching his black beard, "if only I could get an axe which wouldn't break."

As he said this, his mind dimmed as it was by ale, fired up.

He moved to the sitting room and stumbled over to the bookshelf opposite the fireplace. There was a green book on one of the shelves with a worn-out spine and title but Rodgerhath knew it. The book told the tale of Redbeard the greatest dwarf warrior of all time.

Rodgerhath took the book from the shelf and fell back into his comfy chair. He flipped through the pages, past the account of Redbeard's victory over the dragon of the Mountain Hall, his battle with the stone giants and his journey across the distant sea. Rodgerhath skipped to the end of the book and to the chapter on Redbeard's death.

Redbeard had fallen to the fangs of a great serpent in a grove below the White Mountain, a great peak of white rock and stone in the middle of an otherwise level forest.

Rodgerhath's eyes glazed over the text and straight to the illustration. The black and white drawing depicted Redbeard lying on the ground in a pool of his own blood. Next to the mighty warrior lay a weapon and Rodgerhath tapped it with a drunken finger.

"That! That is what I need!"

It was the Goldenaxe.

This weapon had seen the hands of hundreds of great warriors; some famous but others forgotten to time. It was said to be unbreakable, un-scratchable, and ever keen and ever sharp.

Redbeard was the last dwarf to wield the legendary axe. Although his body had been found and buried, the axe with which he slew the serpent was never found. Some said that the great serpent had done the unthinkable and destroyed the weapon. Other more hopeful dwarves claimed the axe had left Redbeard and was now seeking the next great dwarf warrior to aid him in his battles.

But others said that the axe was still somewhere around the White Mountain but hundreds of dwarfs had scoured the grove and the nearby mountain over the centuries and never found it.

Despite the differing accounts of the axe's whereabouts, Rodgerhath decided in his ale-happy state that he should try to find the Goldenaxe.

He put the book back on the shelf and went to the front door, picking up the shaft of his headless axe.

Then he stopped.

Although he was drunk, he knew he'd have to take some provisions for his quest.

He walked back from the front door to the cellar door. He descended the steps and considered his collection of ales on the shelves before him.

"Gold, stout, brown, bitter, pale, cloudy…" he murmured in deep deliberation, "I shall go for the gold."

He pulled a keg of golden ale off the shelf and placed it under one arm and made to leave the cellar but stopped.

"Ah and just one cheeky porter."

He took a dark bottle of black stout off another rack with his free hand and pulled the cork out with his teeth and took a mighty swig.

He sighed with satisfaction and marched up the cellar steps and to his front door to embark upon his grand quest leaving his axe shaft behind.

*

Rodgerhath awoke with a splitting headache and ringing ears.

He opened his blurry eyes but didn't move otherwise because part of him hoped the hangover would pass over if he lay completely still.

Even with his groggy eyes, Rodgerhath got the impression that the ceiling of his bedroom was higher than before. He couldn't remember going into his bedroom but he knew he would have returned to the house at some stage.

As sensation returned to his now heavy and weary body, he felt an unusual soreness across his back and neck.

That's odd, I bought a new mattress recently, he thought. But it feels like I'm sleeping on naked metal.

He moved a hand to rub his eyes and felt his arm brush some metal objects beneath him followed by distinctive clinking sounds.

With mounting confusion, Rodgerhath rubbed his eyes and lifted his lead-heavy and pulsating head to look at what he was lying on in the dim light.

He saw three things.

The first was that he was not in his bed, but instead lying on a gigantic heap of gold coins.

The second was he wasn't in his bedroom or even his house; he was in some vast, gloomy cavern and stalactites and stalagmites were everywhere. Burning torches were mounted on the stalagmites and provided orange light around the chamber.

The third was his keg and bottle were missing and his right hand was holding an axe.

An axe made of pure gold.

Rodgerhath froze, his mind cleared and focused, the pain and mental fog temporarily gone.

5

It couldn't be but yet…

He staggered to his feet, ignoring the pile of gold coins and looked around for a suitable target, something hard and solid.

One of the walls of the cavern was twenty feet away, there was a crude stone shelf carved into it and a solid steel helm was resting on it. Rodgerhath dragged his heavy legs towards the helmet. When he had closed the distance, he adjusted his stance and raised the axe above his head. The weapon felt magical, its balance was perfect and its shaft fitted into his hands like a glove.

Rodgerhath's strike, although poorly executed due to his hangover, was powerful and mighty. The axe cut straight through the helmet as if it were butter and cracked the stone shelf as if it had been nothing harder than a clay pot.

The axe struck with force and the clang echoed throughout the cavern and was so loud, Rodgerhath dropped it and brought his palms to his ears which were not ready for such noise.

When the echoes had ceased, Rodgerhath looked at the dropped weapon.

There wasn't a mark on it.

Rodgerhath gasped and he almost fell to the floor, shock overawing him.

It was the Goldenaxe!

Chapter Two

Rodgerhath couldn't believe his eyes. He had found the Goldenaxe. He had found it.

He couldn't help but chuckle, joy and reverence flooded through him as he picked up the axe with shaking hands.

Just wait till Flowergem sees this and Stronghath and Goldhelm! Oh, Goldhelm will go green with envy!

Rodgerhath's mirth was high and strong but it was not powerful enough to overwhelm the fear he felt as the nature of his situation dawned on him. He was alone in some cavern underground...

And he had no idea how he had got there.

He could remember leaving the house with his beer but he couldn't remember how he had arrived in this cave or how he had found the Goldenaxe. The events after he'd passed over his doorstep were not a blur; they just didn't exist. His memory was completely blank.

This worried him. What was more troubling was he didn't know where he was now and someone or some creature had to tend to the torches in the chamber.

He had no idea if he was safe or whether the creatures who lived here were dangerous.

Rodgerhath forced these worries out of his mind. Worry was not going to help him, only action would be of aid.

Ignoring his drumming head, aching muscles and the desire to lie down and wait for the hangover to pass, he moved around the cavern looking for an exit. He found only one tunnel, he did not know where it led but it was his only option.

Rodgerhath moved slowly through the gloomy tunnel partly out of caution and partly because of his throbbing head. He had the Goldenaxe ready but he knew he was not prepared for a fight and it would be best to avoid violence if possible.

It's possible there's nothing dangerous here, he thought to himself, but he knew deep down this was unlikely. He'd been sleeping on a pile of gold coins and it was unlikely they had arrived there by accident or that the person who had piled them was benevolent.

As he continued up the tunnel, he realized intuitively that it had been made by something other than the forces of nature. Some creature or creatures had chiselled and mined their way through the rock with crude tools.

Wherever this passage led, Rodgerhath knew it wouldn't be as safe as he hoped.

The tunnel wound on for what seemed to be hundreds of yards to Rodgerhath's booze-addled head but if he had been sober, he'd only have judged it to number fifty. The passage twisted through rugged rock before ending in another cavern – torches hung by entrances revealing a honeycomb of tunnels and underground pathways.

A chill crept down Rodgerhath's spine and his dry mouth became even more arid. He recognized the structure of these tunnels and the strange odour that had been irritating his nostrils, he was in the lair of a tribe of…

"Trogs!"

Startled by the command, Rodgerhath ducked behind the corner of a nearby passage to hide himself from the creature which was trampling down the main tunnel. He sensed motion from some of the other smaller tunnels and chambers.

"Trogs!" the voice bellowed and again the echoes grew louder as the brutish voice drew closer.

As much as Rodgerhath was willing to dare, he peeked around the edge of the passage to see what was happening.

Lumbering down the tunnel was a creature with skin as grey as stone and as tough as old leather, its face was a mess of black hair, pierced by yellow eyes and from which protruded a large potato-shaped nose.

He was a trog. A mighty trog, three heads taller than the tallest man Rodgerhath had ever met. He was nearly the width of two men with tree trunk arms that reached his knobbly knees and with great hands which could swallow a man's face in their grip.

The thewy and muscular monster was wearing nought but a large loin-cloth around his waist which was made of cave moss and draped across his wide shoulders was a bearskin poorly ripped and treated from the unfortunate beast.

Atop the head of the cave dweller was a crown of bright shining gold, but Rodgerhath could tell that it wasn't trogish metallurgy that had crafted such a fine ornament. Trogs were raiders and this beautiful crown was no doubt a spoil of war or a "warspoil" as they liked to call them.

From the other passages, Rodgerhath could see the shapes of different trogs coming to the shouts of the crowned one. They were stout and stocky, shorter and less powerful than the tall one who was clearly their king.

Rodgerhath drew back and listened closely, his head pounding, his body sweating and the Goldenaxe resting at his side.

"Warboss, what is it?" a voice grunted.

"Warclubs!" the deep voice commanded, ignoring the question. "Nug was attacked on watch duty. We have an invader!"

"Attacked by what?"

"Something short and weak I imagine. Nug is such a weed that any weakling thing can beat him!" another trog shouted.

There was a roar of loud laughter from the trogs and Rodgerhath had to cover his ears to stop his head splitting open.

The warboss bellowed and the laughter stopped, only its echoes touched the ears.

"Whoever hurts one of us, hurts all of us. No matter how weak. Get your warclubs! Whoever gets this invader will keep his warspoils!"

This command and promise of plunder excited the battle-hungry trogs into action. Rodgerhath heard them charge through the tunnels to get their weapons and start hunting...

Chapter Three

Flowergem was unduly disturbed by her husband's absence.

She'd awoken bright and early and realized something was amiss. For one, she couldn't smell any beery breath in the bedroom and second Rodgerhath could not be found next to her sleeping soundly. In fact, there were no signs Rodgerhath had ever returned to the bed.

Flowergem got up and began to search the house for him, at times he had passed out in the garden, the cellar and even in the living room but she couldn't find him anywhere.

With growing tension, she went outside and searched around the whole village, she checked all the usual and unusual spots but her husband was nowhere to be found.

Once she knew Rodgerhath was truly missing she went to Goldhelm's house and knocked on his door interrupting his breakfast.

"What is it?" Goldhelm grunted as he opened the door. The captain of the dwarven militia hated mealtime interruptions.

"Rodgerhath was drinking last night…"

"Is there a night he doesn't?"

"He's not here!" Flowergem cried, "I can't find him anywhere."

*

After finishing his breakfast, Goldhelm called together a search party. It included a dozen of the guard, Flowergem and her father Culbert. They knew Rodgerhath wasn't in the village so they made their way to the front gate and searched around the fortified walls of the hamlet but he was nowhere to be found.

So the party returned to the front gate and Goldhelm examined the ground. He said nothing for a long minute before throwing his arms up in frustration.

"It's hopeless!" he said, "there are tracks everywhere. All the farmers and their livestock have moved early this morning."

Flowergem's heart dropped. She sensed her husband was in danger and she knew that they had to find him, but it wasn't possible to begin searching without an idea of where he had been going.

Before she could express her fears, she saw her father drop to one knee and begin sniffing the path.

"What are you…?" Goldhelm began.

Culbert raised a hand and continued to sniff.

"Ale," he said.

"Ale? You can smell ale? How? The wind is clean and sober!" Goldhelm exclaimed.

"Yes… it's one of my pale ales… my dandelion ale! Yes that's the one, he must have been drinking and spilling it wherever he was going."

"Is there a trail father?" Flowergem asked daring to hope.

Culbert got to his feet and walked up the path still sniffing the air.

"That there is! Follow me!"

Chapter Four

Rodgerhath now knew where he was or, at least, he thought he knew where he was.

He could now remember that he had decided to go to the White Mountain to search for the Goldenaxe. Knowing what he knew about trogs and their tendency to make their strongholds in caves and caverns, he realized he was inside the White Mountain.

However, he couldn't figure out how the trog tunnels had not been found years before. Dwarves had scoured the grove and the mountain in search of the Goldenaxe and never encountered trogs.

Either the trogs were recent arrivals or they had remained hidden for all those years. Regardless, it raised a question which confounded him: how did he manage to discover the trogs' warriordom in his drunken condition?

Rodgerhath was in trouble because he couldn't answer this question. If he could answer it, he would know how he managed to enter the trogs' warriordom and then he would know how to escape. As it was, he would be going through the passages blind looking for the exit.

He listened closely and considered his options. The trogs appeared to have gone but they would probably make their way back but they were searching the other tunnels for him at the moment. This meant everywhere was dangerous.

After rubbing his eyes and brushing his forehead in an attempt to relieve the pains of his hangover, Rodgerhath decided he had to make a move. He wasn't going to wait to be hunted down like a dog, if he was going to die, he wanted to die standing and in a battle of his own choosing.

"I'm going to get out of here or I'm going to die trying!" he told himself.

Forcing his head up, resting the Goldenaxe on his shoulder and lifting his legs, Rodgerhath moved in a groggy fashion out of his hiding place and into the main tunnel.

Rodgerhath had a choice, he could either go left or right. Left would take him where the trogs had gone searching for him but right would take him away from them.

After a second of thought, Rodgerhath went left. He reasoned that because the warboss had come from that direction and, because all the trogs had gone up that passage searching for him, the exit out of the White Mountain had to be that way.

He knew that this was the dangerous route and that he could easily find himself face-to-face with a trog or even a whole war band. But there was nothing for it, he had to try and escape.

"As long as they don't shout too loudly, I might be able to fight my way through a couple of them," Rodgerhath mumbled to himself, too loudly to be stealthy. Fortunately, there were no trogs around to hear him and he continued up the passage undisturbed.

For the first dozen yards it was a straight cavern with multiple small chambers to the right and left which were the sleeping dens of the trogs and their broods. As Rodgerhath continued up the passage, the dens disappeared and the cavern began to twist and turn and wiggle through the black rock.

After travelling a couple hundred yards, the tunnel split into five separate passageways, two went leftward, one continued straight and the last two went rightward.

Rodgerhath listened closely to gauge how many trogs had gone down each tunnel but his ears were still muffled due to last night's merriment and he wasn't sure whether he was hearing faint trog echoes or whether he was just imagining these things.

He now had to make another decision: which tunnel to take.

Rodgerhath thought back to the cavern in which he had first awoken. Because it was a natural chamber with no exits other than the one the trogs had made, it occurred to Rodgerhath that the trogs had been mining deeper and further into the mountain.

Therefore, he reasoned, if he went in the opposite direction of the natural cavern, he would find his way out of the mountain. His headache briefly relented with the surge of serotonin that this thought granted, and he moved down the first rightward tunnel and prayed that his hunch would prove correct.

Rodgerhath held the Goldenaxe at the ready, he kept his eyes and ears focused ahead even though it hurt his throbbing head to do so. Sweat prickled across his hot skin as his emotions wrestled with the anticipation of combat.

Thoughts about his neighbours, his friends and his wife flooded his mind. How would they react if he didn't return? There would be much sadness and many tears; he could see it playing out in front of him. Rodgerhath could see Flowergem at the head of a solemn procession, dressed in black, tears falling down already wet cheeks.

Rodgerhath snapped his mind from this vision back to the present. It was doing him no favours to entertain the worst case scenario, he needed to focus on the situation as it was.

"Besides I'm not going to die," Rodgerhath decided, "I'm going to make it home and tell her how much she means to me... and then I'm getting a celebratory pint!"

At that moment, his head chose to throb badly with pain.

"Err... I might do that one another day."

Aside from these ill-tempered mutterings, Rodgerhath continued up the tunnel in silence.

And "up" was the appropriate preposition, the tunnel was gently sloping upwards and continued for what felt like an eternity until it ended in a stone spiral staircase which went straight up.

Rodgerhath was impressed, it was a crude construction with uneven steps but he was surprised the trogs had been able to craft a functional stairway. They were such dumb brutes obsessed with war and violence that they often never bothered with learning any of the fine crafts.

Maybe these stairs lead out of this mountain, Rodgerhath thought.

He began to ascend the steps, carefully and deliberately as they were so uneven that one poorly considered foot would cause him to trip and fall.

The unorthodox movements necessitated by the stairway's poor construction, paired with the concentration required to climb the ever-spiralling stairs, made Rodgerhath's headache even worse and twice he felt like vomiting.

Somehow, Rodgerhath kept it all together and reached the last step where he promptly collapsed onto one of the cavern walls to get his breath back and rest his turbulent stomach.

After a minute of rest, Rodgerhath felt healthy enough to move again. He looked up and examined the chamber which he was now in.

He froze. Lined up against the walls and lying in piles on the floor were dozens of trog warclubs. All were made of crudely carved rough stone and looked unwieldy but heavy.

There were no trogs in the chamber to grab these clubs and Rodgerhath calmed his beating heart. He had been trained as a warrior and control of his heart and emotions was second nature to him.

He examined the chamber carefully, although nothing was organized in a manner easy to comprehend with a dwarf's eye, he could tell that the trogs had been into the chamber recently and taken some of them. Clearly, the trogs liked having spares.

Rodgerhath nodded approvingly. This was something he could understand.

He saw on the other side of the warclub room a tunnel and from it he could feel a breeze hitting his skin.

Hope surged within Rodgerhath as he imagined the outside world at its end. He trudged through the warclubs and up the tunnel expecting to see sunlight at its end.

However, no such light was forth coming but there was the sense of a wide open expanse ahead. As Rodgerhath neared the end of the tunnel, he saw that he was coming onto a ledge which was overlooking a massive cavern. He could hear talking echoing from below. Keeping low, he moved out of the tunnel onto the ledge and looked below.

The wide open cavern met his eyes and he saw a hundred foot drop. At the other end of the vast chamber was what looked like a stone gate, although "gate" was too grand a term for what was essentially a large boulder pressed against the wall with the word "door" carved into it.

In the centre of the cavern was the trog warboss and several other trogs, one of whom was on the ground moaning and rubbing his head.

"That hurt!" the one on the ground cried.

"And it will hurt some more unless you tell me where he went!" the warboss growled. "Where did he go, Nug?"

"I don't know boss, honest! I was by the door as you ordered. I just opened it for a tinkle and as I turned, this dwarf pops out of nowhere calls me a "rough-necked, slime-licking, piddle-block-head" and smacked me over the head with this."

He lifted up a plank of curved wood and Rodgerhath recognized it. It was what remained of his beer keg.

"And...?" the warboss asked, expectantly.

"...I can't remember anything else... he hit me very hard."

The warboss struck the kneeling trog on the head.

"Owww!"

"Maybe that will help you remember!"

Two trogs ran out into view resting their clubs on their shoulders.

"We've searched the northern chambers and found no trace of the dwarf."

"Bah! Useless! The lot of you!" the warboss cried.

As the conversation continued below him, Rodgerhath considered his options. He'd have to go back down the stairs the way he had come if he wanted to reach the gate below. He would have to wait until...

"There he is!"

Rodgerhath spun around and saw two angry trogs appear at the entrance to the ledge.

"Get him!"

The brutes charged, clubs ready to swing.

Rodgerhath scrambled to his feet and managed to doge the first club but he lost his footing...

He yelled as he tumbled over the ledge, the Goldenaxe slipped from his grip as he entered freefall.

Chapter Five

It turned out that while there was a hundred foot drop below the ledge, Rodgerhath hadn't actually been standing on a steep cliff. His hungover eyes couldn't see it but there was a rocky slope underneath the ledge which continued all the way to the floor of the cavern.

Rodgerhath hit this slope and the world spun as he rolled down the rocky incline, his limbs and back battered into sore numbness. He twirled and tumbled in this painful manner for what seemed like an eternity before he hit something and halted abruptly.

Reeling from the rolling and this sudden impact, Rodgerhath tried to make sense of his surroundings but his vision was blurred and his eyes couldn't focus on anything. The whole world still seemed to be spinning.

He thought he could hear talking, in fact, he knew there was talking but his ears couldn't make head or tail of what was being said.

Rodgerhath forced himself up and leaned against the stalagmite he had crashed into. Blinking as fast as he could, he tried to restore his vision but all he could see in between blinks was vague surroundings and a shape approaching him.

Adrenaline kicked his eyes back into focus as the shape reached out a hand and grabbed him by the collar.

"Well what have we here?" the trog warboss growled.

Rodgerhath tried grabbing the thumbs and fingers of the trog in attempt to twist and break them. But the warboss' grip was too tight and his fingers were too strong for such a move to work.

"The warspoils are mine!"

The warboss lifted his warclub with his free hand.

Rodgerhath began striking the arm holding his collar but the trog didn't even flinch, his hold and grip remained firm and did not yield.

Rodgerhath would have died right there, his skull crushed by the stone club of the warboss, but tumbling down a cave slope after drinking enough beer to down three men is not something anyone - man, dwarf or trog - should do.

Rodgerhath in one last desperate attempt grabbed one of the trog king's fingers with both hands and pulled on it. He managed to pull the finger from his throat, allowing air into his lungs and for the contents of his stomach to well up.

He vomited right in the trog's face who dropped him immediately.

"Ugh!" the warboss recoiled, dropping his club so he could use both hands to wipe the puke off his face.

Rodgerhath landed on his feet and, not wasting a second, rushed and shoved the trog with both arms. The warboss tumbled backwards tripping over his club.

"Don't just stand there! Get him!" the warboss commanded as he hit the ground.

The three trogs who had been behind the warboss raised their clubs.

Rodgerhath glanced around searching for a weapon, then he saw the Goldenaxe gleaming next to a nearby stalagmite. He ran over to it and lifted it just as the first trog drew into striking range.

The trog swung at Rodgerhath, it was a downward strike and the dwarf easily side-stepped it. Then with an arching swing of his own, Rodgerhath struck the trog in the ribcage.

The trog's chest collapsed as the axe split through the ribs and ruptured internal organs. He fell over and hit the ground, the fight taken from him as his rancid soul entered the void.

The second trog was taken aback by Rodgerhath's clean kill but he paused for only a second before bellowing a war cry and charging at the dwarf.

The trog looked as if he were going for a rightward swing and Rodgerhath jumped back as the brute advanced.

But it was a feint.

With deft skill, the trog lifted the club above his head and brought it down. Rodgerhath cursed, he should have guessed, trogs always preferred downward strikes. He lifted the Goldenaxe with both arms to block the blow.

And block it, the Goldenaxe did.

The club slammed into the haft of the legendary axe and went no further. Rodgerhath tilted the weapon and caught the club with the axe head. He pulled the stone club out of the trog's hands and, bringing the axe back, he struck the brute in the neck.

With a spray of blood, the trog's head came clean off and it hit the ground and bounced just as gravity pulled down the lifeless body to which it had belonged.

The third trog, Nug, upon seeing his two comrades so quickly and brutally taken down by a single hungover dwarf, turned and fled.

"Nug!" the warboss bellowed, now back on his feet, "I always knew you were a whelp!"

With one hand, the warboss swung his club at Nug's head.

There was a loud crack as Nug's head rolled back and his heavy body struck the ground as his life stopped.

By now, many other trogs had arrived at the scene but they stood back and watched as their chieftain faced Rodgerhath.

"You're mine!" he snarled, "or my name's not Trug!"

Rodgerhath readied himself, the warboss Trug was taller and stronger than the two trogs he had killed and he guessed that he was more aggressive and battle seasoned.

Trug stepped forwards, slowly and deliberately, his muscles loose and relaxed but his eyes focused and fierce. Rodgerhath looked around him quickly, he could see the stone gate which led to the outside world but he wouldn't be able to reach it, let alone open it, before the warboss was on top of him. He was in this fight and there was only one way out of it.

The warboss was burning with battle hunger yet he did not charge, instead, he stepped to the side attempting to move in a different direction to flank Rodgerhath. The dwarf responded by stepping to the other side and so the two began to circle one another.

As they circled, they drew closer. Trug stepped closer out of a raw primal urge to kill the dwarf who had invaded his warriordom and Rodgerhath edged closer because the only way out was through.

Then with a sudden yell, Trug swung his heavy warclub. Rodgerhath jumped to the side and swung the Goldenaxe at the trog but the warboss leaned back nimbly dodging the strike.

The trogs erupted with hollering and shouting which split Rodgerhath's already aching head.

Rodgerhath was disorientated, pained and angry. The anger and the frustration which come from pain rarely have any suitable outlet at the best of times but at this worst of times Rodgerhath was able to channel them on to one target.

He snarled, catching the trog leader off-guard and leapt at him, the Goldenaxe swinging. Trug had not expected the assault and he was caught flat-footed. He stumbled in his retreat and so was not poised to riposte or dodge an attack and Rodgerhath, even at half his mental strength, saw an opening.

The dwarf struck the trog in his side, the Goldenaxe bit deeply into Trug's ribs and stomach.

Next second Rodgerhath felt Trug's fist meet his face and he span backwards, the axe still in his grip as he recoiled from the blow. He felt blood explode from his crunched and broken nose and his vision blurred as he stumbled backwards, his head throbbing.

Rodgerhath had not seen Trug let go of the club with his left hand and did not have a chance to evade or block the strike. But the warboss was worse for wear, Trug was gasping for air and staggering from Rodgerhath's own strike, blood gushing from his wound.

This blow would have taken down a lesser trog but Trug was the warboss of the White Mountain and was from a long line of brutish chieftains.

Trug gripped his club with both hands, roared loudly, breaking the cold silence of the cavern and charged at Rodgerhath, his eyes ablaze with bloodlust as he was possessed by a berserker's rage.

Rodgerhath's heart sank in fear.

Trug swung violently, what little form he had was gone as he thrashed at Rdogerhath with all his might and fury. Rodgerhath was in full retreat but he kept control and did not turn his back to the trog as this would have been certain death.

The assault was short but powerful in its intensity. The fast strides, the powerful strikes which never hit home and the quick movements left Trug weakened. His wound tore further and his body ripped itself. Lifeblood poured from his already mortal wound and soon he was coughing up the same blood which was dripping from his side.

Then his rage finally failed him.

Trug fell to his knees, his club slipped from his fingers and he coughed up more lifeblood. Still, he kept his head high and from behind he must have looked defiant to his underlings. Indeed, there was defiance in Trug but his face expressed something else. His eyes looked into Rodgerhath's own and pleaded. They begged for a clean death, an honourable death free from the disgrace and pain of dying outside the battlefield – a death delivered from one warrior to another.

Rodgerhath made the slightest nod.

Gripping the Goldenaxe with both hands, he charged and raised the legendary weapon high and Trug closed his eyes. With a clean swing the axe went down onto Trug's chest and into his heart.

Bone cracked and flesh tore but Trug the warboss smiled before he rolled over and his spirit fell into oblivion.

As Trug's body fell onto the ground lifeless, Rodgerhath saw the faces in the crowd of trogs change from to shock to terror. Rodgerhath took a step towards them and they turned tail and ran howling in fright like beaten dogs.

Convinced they would bother him no longer, Rodgerhath turned and walked to the stone gate.

Chapter Six

Flowergem and the rest of the search party looked at the base of the White Mountain. Culbert was right next to the white rock face, he walked up and down sniffing the air.

He did this for a few seconds before looking at the cliff and scratching his bald head.

"I don't get it," he said, "the trail ends here."

Goldhelm stepped forwards and examined the ground.

"Someone has been here," he said, "but I can't see where he went."

Flowergem felt cold.

"He has to be around here somewhere," she said, "maybe he went up the mountain?"

"I'll lead a team up the mountain," Goldhelm said, "Flowergem, you should lead another group around the base. Who will come with me and who will go with Flowergem?"

The group was about to split into halves when there was the sound of a dull thud. They heard and felt it, minor as the impact was.

The dwarves went silent and listened, the same noise was heard but this time it was louder. They could detect where it was coming from now: the rock wall ahead of them where Culbert was still standing.

The thuds continued and Culbert placed his ear to the rock wall to investigate further. The thuds grew stronger, harder and louder until…

Crack!

A golden blade punctured through the white rock inches away from Culbert's face. He fell backwards and crawled back seven feet, his eyes wide and his jaw chattering.

The rest of the dwarves readied their weapons and looked to the axe which was chipping the hole to make it bigger. It was extraordinary, the axe was made of gold yet it did not bend or break as it carved through the white stone.

The dwarves watched in amazement and then a chorus of dwarven voices exclaimed all at once: "It's the Goldenaxe!"

"The Goldenaxe!"

"It's the Goldenaxe!"

"It's my ale!"

Culbert was scrambling to his feet and sniffing the air.

"It's my ale! It's Rodgerhath!"

"Please not so loud!" a familiar voice cried.

Everyone went silent.

"I have a terrible headache."

"Husband!"

Flowergem rushed towards the head-shaped, and sized, gap in the stone.

"Wife!"

Flowergem poked her head through the hole and saw Rodgerhath in front of her. He looked tired, he was drenched with sweat, his nose was broken and bleeding but he was very much alive.

Flowergem pushed herself forwards and kissed him.

"My darling, you're hurt!"

"Only a flesh wound. I'm very thirsty and I need to lie down. But stand back my dear. This door will not open for all of my shoving and pulling. I need to break myself out of this place."

Flowergem moved from the hole and Rodgerhath set the Goldenaxe to work once more. In ten short minutes, he and the axe had made an opening big enough for him to squeeze through.

Upon stepping into the bright daylight, he was set upon by Flowergem who hugged him tight and Goldhelm who offered a bottle of water and a handkerchief. Rodgerhath drank deeply from the bottle and sighed with happiness; never had pure water tasted so good.

As he wiped the blood off his face, the other dwarves stood around in a wide circle and stared wide-eyed at the Goldenaxe in Rodgerhath's hand. At first, the dwarves held back their curiosity and amazement but after a minute they lost all self-control and unleashed their burning questions.

"Is that the Goldenaxe?"

"Where did you get it?"

"How did you get it?"

"Please!" Rodgerhath cried.

The crowd went silent again.

"I'll answer your very reasonable and understandable questions later. Right now I just want to go home. And then tomorrow…"

He paused for dramatic effect.

"I'll visit Stronghath and show him my new axe!"

The End
Edward White

Printed in Great Britain
by Amazon

32809955R00018